Ship to:

THE FABULOUS
BOUNCING CHOWDER

From: The Snarf Snack Company

Peter Brown

LITTLE, BROWN AND COMPANY
New York · Boston

For Doc

ALSO BY PETER BROWN:
Flight of the Dodo
Chowder

Little, Brown and Company

Hachette Book Group USA
237 Park Avenue, New York, NY 10017
Visit our Web site at www.lb-kids.com

First Edition: September 2007

ISBN-13: 978-0-316-01179-2
ISBN-10: 0-316-01179-7

10 9 8 7 6 5 4 3 2 1

SC

Manufactured in China

The illustrations for this book were done in acrylic and pencil on board.
The text was set in Nimrod, and the display type is Kon Tiki.

Chowder knew they were just avoiding him.

One morning after breakfast, Ms. Fabu made a special **announcement**.

"We are going to have our own official dog show!" she said. "You little darlings will be competing in the *First Annual Fabu Pooch Pageant*! So start preparing and remember that the only way to fetch your fabulousness is to follow your dreams!"

Chowder knew he was kind of funny-looking. It was difficult enough being surrounded by perfect dogs, but competing against them just seemed like a lost cause.

"Oh, I almost forgot," added Ms. Fabu,
"the winner will get a one-year supply of
delicious Snarf Snacks!"

Now she was speaking Chowder's language.
Snarf Snacks were a true doggy delicacy.
Just one shake of the box and hounds from
all over could be heard howling with hunger.
He didn't know how he'd do it, but Chowder
was determined to win that prize!

The campers got right down to business.
Lola spent a few weeks working on her
TOOTHY GRIN.

Snapper went to a canine chiropractor.

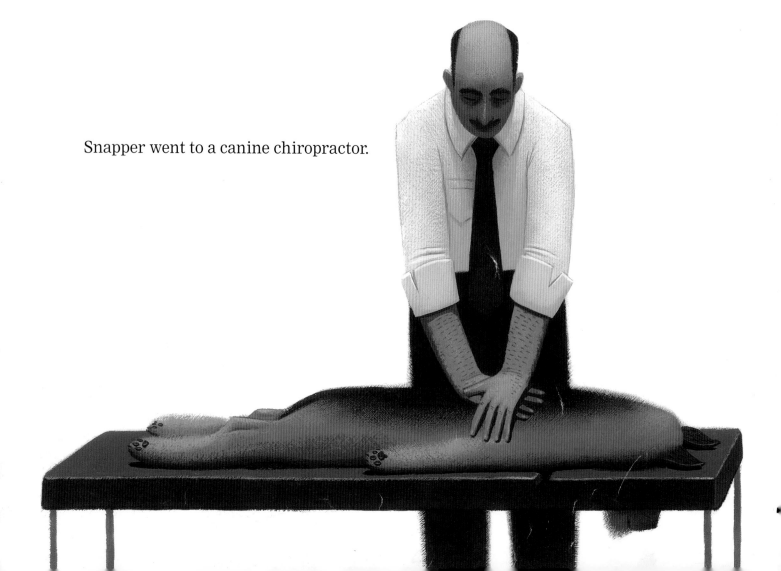

And Beverly got a perm.

All of the dogs were looking more and more like
CHAMPIONS—all of them except Chowder.

Chowder *tried* to make himself a bit more *fabulous*.
But he needed a new plan.

One day, while watching TV with the Wubbingtons,
Chowder saw a commercial for Twisty's Acrobatic Fanatic Camp.
He **dreamed** of going there, but Twisty would *not* allow dogs.
So Madge and Bernie turned to a dear old friend for help.

Ms. Shirley Fabu ran the Fabu Pooch Boot Camp.
Her specialty was turning beautiful dogs into fabulous dogs.
They went on field trips to dog shows and dog salons, and they
sharpened their skills in fabulousness.

The Wubbingtons thought that Chowder would enjoy it there, but as usual, he didn't quite fit in.

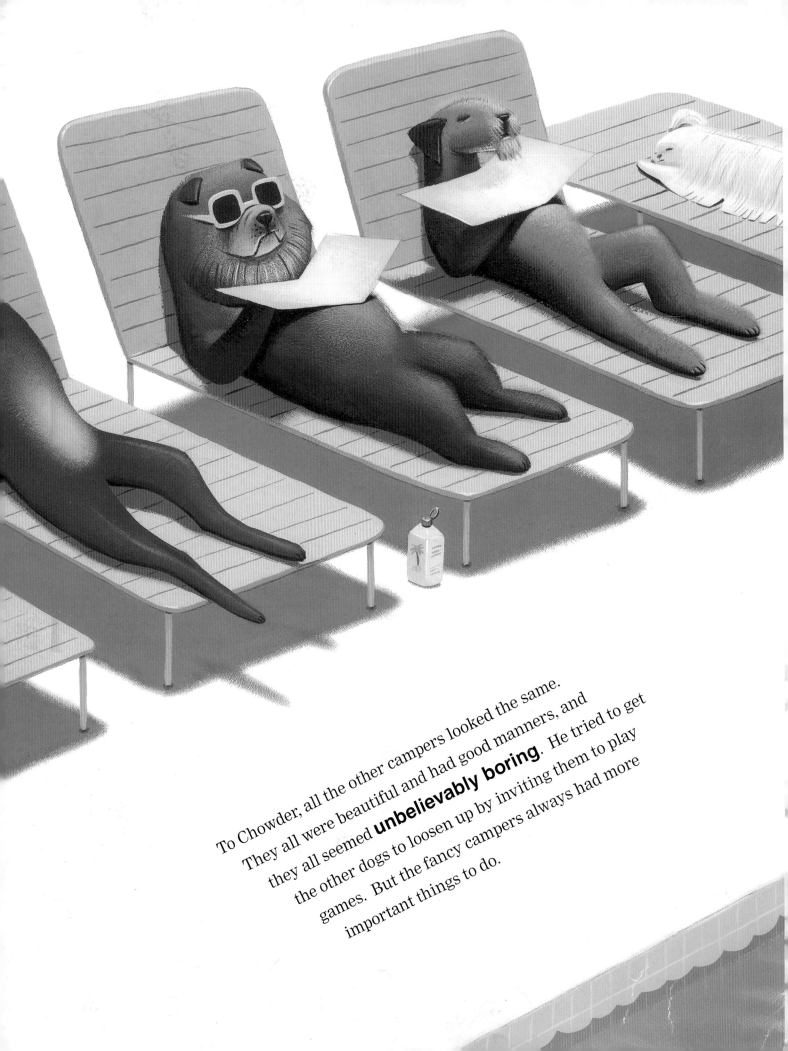

To Chowder, all the other campers looked the same. They all were beautiful and had good manners, and they all seemed **unbelievably boring**. He tried to get the other dogs to loosen up by inviting them to play games. But the fancy campers always had more important things to do.

Ms. Fabu always told the campers to follow their dreams, and Chowder had a lot of dreams to choose from. He dreamed of being a professional kickball player, an astronaut, a gourmet chef—the list went on. But Chowder's greatest dream was to be an acrobat, and when his curiosity led him behind the barn things began to look up.

It was **love** at first sight. Chowder climbed onto the old trampoline, brushed it off, and began bouncing around.

He was a natural.

While Beverly was primping, Chowder became **ONE** with the trampoline.

As Snapper perfected his posture, Chowder studied the great masters.

During one of Lola's many flossing sessions,
Chowder tried to **lick** the moon.

Before they knew it, the day of the **Fabu Pooch Pageant** had arrived. Droves of dogs and people from far and wide came to see the up-and-coming canines in their first competition. Even Chowder had a few fans in the crowd.

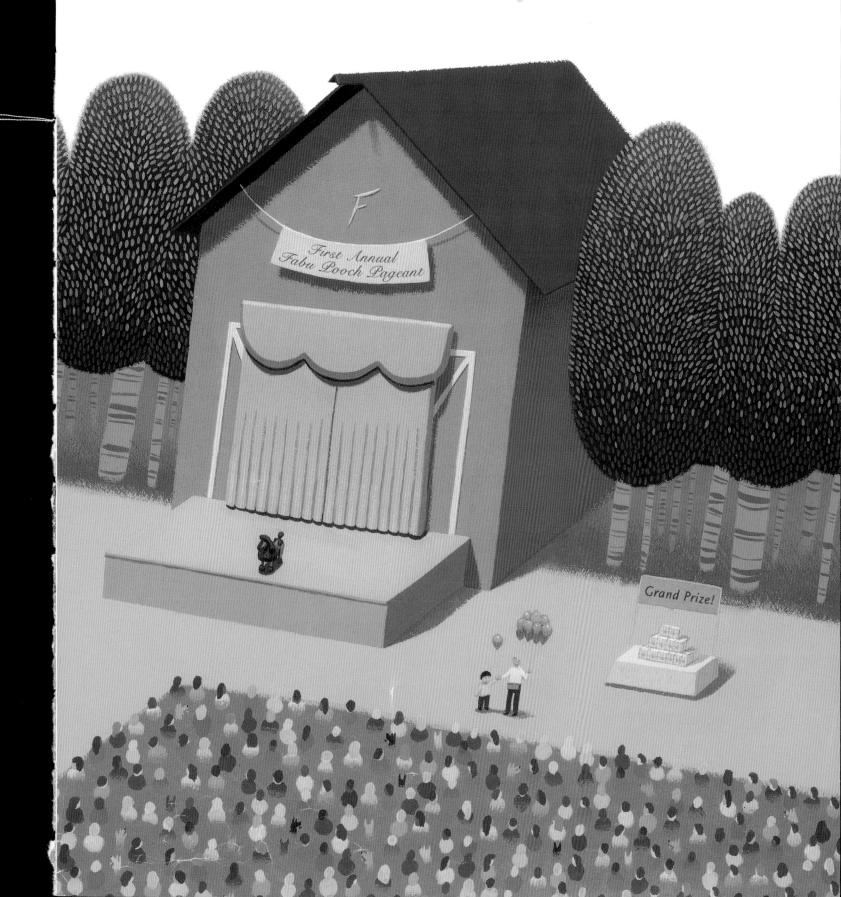

All the other campers were in top form.
Lola's smile was sparkling.

Beverly's hair was breathtaking.

Snapper's posture was superb.

Finally it was time for Chowder. The curtains
opened to reveal nothing but the old trampoline.
The crowd was growing restless when suddenly
they heard a **bark** from above!

"YEEEEOOOOWWW!"

Chowder dove from the roof of the barn,

landed in the center of the trampoline,

and bounced high into the air.

He fell back to the trampoline,
spinning in a tight corkscrew . . .

then he bounced into a flying cartwheel . . .

then three backward flips . . .

. . . and then something he called
"The **Chowderian** Bounce!"

When Chowder finished his routine, the crowd went crazy!
The sounds of cheering and barking and *mooing* and
oinking rolled forward like a tidal wave.

Ms. Fabu clapped harder than anyone. "Chowder,
that was *SO FABULOUS*!" she cheered.

The judges loved Chowder's bounce-tacular performance,
but it really didn't belong in a competition like the Fabu Pooch Pageant.
So instead of giving him the top prize, they gave him the honorary award of
Best Bouncer in Show.

Chowder was quite proud of himself.

Beverly may have gotten the year's supply of Snarf Snacks, but Chowder became the official spokesdoggy of the Snarf Snacks Company. And for that he received a *lifetime* supply of his favorite treats!

The following summer Ms. Fabu
insisted that Chowder return to her camp.

And when he got there, Chowder had a class of
BEGINNING BOUNCERS
eagerly awaiting their first lesson.